Métis Christmas Mittens
Lii Mitenn Michif di Nowel

Written and illustrated by Leah Marie Dorion

Michif translation by Norman Fleury

Library and Archives Canada Cataloguing in Publication

Dorion, Leah, 1970-, author, illustrator
    Métis Christmas mittens = Lii mitenn Michif di Nowel / written and illustrated by Leah Marie Dorion ; Michif translation by Norman Fleury.

Text in English and Michif.
ISBN 978-1-926795-79-9 (paperback)

    I. Fleury, Norman, translator II. Dorion, Leah, 1970- . Métis Christmas mittens. III. Dorion, Leah, 1970-. Métis Christmas mittens. Michif. IV. Title. V. Title: Lii mitenn Michif di Nowel.

PS8557.O7483M48 2017   jC813'.6   C2016-907030-1

Gabriel Dumont Institute Press Project Team:

Karon Shmon, Publishing Director and Editor
David Morin, Graphic Designer and Editor
Darren Préfontaine, Editor
Globe Printers, Saskatoon, Printer

Gabriel Dumont Institute Press
2—604 22nd Street West
Saskatoon, SK S7M 5W1
www.gdins.org   www.shopmetis.ca   www.metismuseum.ca

We acknowledge the support of the Canada Council for the Arts, which last year invested $153 million to bring the arts to Canadians throughout the country.

Nous remercions le Conseil des arts du Canada de son soutien. L'an dernier, le Conseil a investi 153 millions de dollars pour mettre de l'art dans la vie des Canadiennes et des Canadiens de tout le pays.

The Gabriel Dumont Institute Press acknowledges the financial support of the Government of Canada for the production and publication of this resource.

Dedicated to my Auntie Isabelle Impey née Dorion,
the seamstress of our entire family.

My family has a Christmas mitten tradition. On cold winter days Métis Christmas mittens are made to warm the hands and the heart.

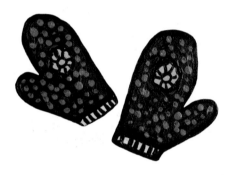

Ma faamii ayaawuk enn tradisyoon di mitenn di Nowel. Lii zhoornii aan nivayr ka kishinaahk lii mitenn Michif di Nowel ooshihikaashoowuk chi kishitayki lii maen pi li keur.

When snow greets the land, Métis families begin to make their special Métis Christmas mittens by hand.

Ishpii la niizh ka pahkishihk disseu la tayr, lii faamii Michif kii maachi ooshihaywuk a la maen lii miiyeur mitenn Michif di Nowel.

Mittens are joyfully worn by every child and adult.

Lii pleu vyeu pi lii zaanfaan kaahkiiyow pootshkawaywuk
lii mitenn avik la zhway.

Métis mittens have been made everywhere across the homeland, from the Red River to the Peace.

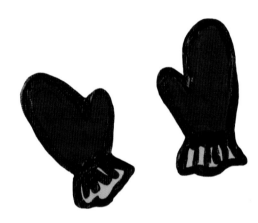

Lii mitenn mishiway kii ooshihikaashoowuk iita lii Michif ka wiikichik, la Rivyayr Roozh ooshchi jusque daan li Peace.

Métis Christmas mittens are made to show we care and to tell others that they belong.

Lii mitenn Michif di Nowel ooshihikaashoowuk chi wapahtaahiwayhk aen pishkayhtamaahk pi chi wiihtamaakayhk enn plaas aen ayayaahk.

Old brown paper mitten patterns, made by grandma's own design, are folded and put in a tin can.

Lii vyeu paatroon brun poor lii mitenn, Noohkoom kayshchiwaak wiiya soon dissayn, napwaykinikaataywa pi daan enn pchit kaan di tool aaschikaatew.

Some Métis mittens are scented with smoked, tanned moose hide. Others are trimmed with beautiful soft beaver fur to calm and comfort the worried mind.

Atiht lii mitenn Michif miiyakooshiwuk avik la bookaan aen kii kiishiniiht. Lii zootr wayshiihaywuk avik la poo di kaastor moo chi kiiyaamayaahk pi chi pishkaapahtamihk ayka chi naakatwayhtamihk daan la mimwayr.

Other Métis Christmas mittens are made from recycled pieces of cloth. This is a reminder to reuse and recycle everything we have and to treat everything with respect.

Lii zootr mitenn Michif di Nowel avik lii morsoo di ginii ooshiikaashoowuk. Chi kishkishiyaahk chi kiitwaam apachistaahk pi ayka chi waypinamaahk ka tipayhtamaahk pi miina kaahkiiyow chi kanawaapahtamihk avik li rispay.

In every stitch, a prayer is made to bring blessings from our caring Creator.

Ita ka kashkiwaashoohk enn priyayr ooshchikaatew chi paytaahk lii binidiksyoon ooshchi nutr Kriiateur ka pishkaymikooyaahk.

Métis Christmas mittens are sewn together by hand using a sharp needle and strong sinew for thread.

Lii mitenn Michif di Nowel kaashkikwaashoowuk aansaamb a la maen avik aen nigwii pwaycheu pi li nayr aen shookuhk poor li fil.

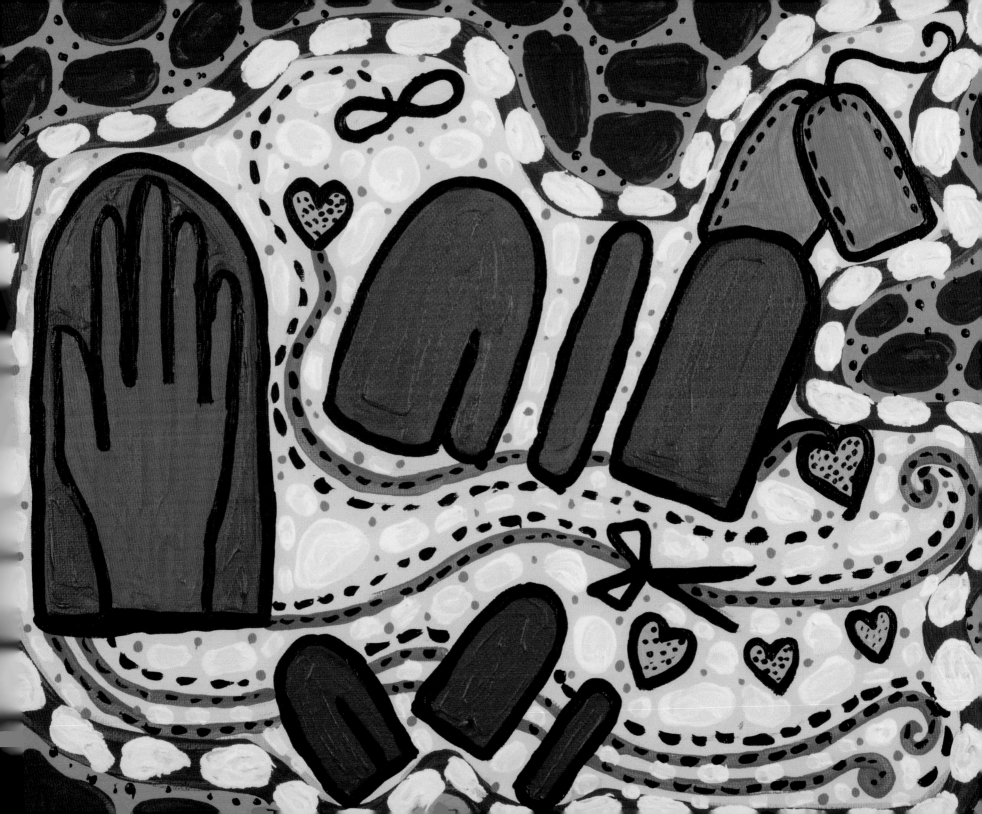

Many are decorated with beautiful flower beadwork, ribbons, and fine embroidery stitches. There are so many different kinds of Métis Christmas mittens!

Mishchayt wayshiishchikaataywa avik lii fleur di rasaad, lii roobaan, loovraazh aen katawashishihk. Mishchayt pi toot sorrt aashtaywa lii mitenn Michif di Nowel.

Pompoms, tassels, and fringes are sometimes added for decoration on our Métis Christmas mittens.

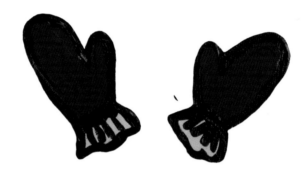

Aashkow lii poopoon, lii glaand, pi lii fraansh takwaashtaawuk aen wayshiihaachik lii mitenn Michif di Nowel.

It was an old Métis tradition to place a small beaded heart on the back of the thumb for good luck and to show love from the maker.

Sitay enn vyay tradisyoon di Michif chi aashtaahk aen pchi keur aan rasaad aan aaryayr li poos poor la bonn luck pi chi waapahtahiwayhk lamoor ooschi ana ka kii ooshihaat.

A touch of beadwork reminds us to live every day connected to our heart.

Aen tashiihkamihk loovraazh di rasaad kishkishoomikoonaan chi pimaatshiyaahk toot lii zhoor aen ayaakwamoohk daan nutr keur.

There are all kinds of Métis mittens, but no two pairs are made exactly the same. Métis people make mittens to give away.

Toot sort di mitenn di Michif ayaawa, maaka namooya deu payr paray ooshihikaashoowuk. Lii Michif ooshihaywuk lii mitenn chi maykihk.

A mitten is rarely lost by a travelling dog team driver. Often, musher's mittens are held together by a brightly-braided cord which runs through their sleeves so they dangle out the jacket arms.

Si raar ka waanihaat sa mitenn ana li chim di shyayn ka pamihaat. Mishchaytwow aniki lii shyayn ka pamihaachik aansaamb leu mitenn tahkoopitaywuk avik enn kord aen apihkaatayk aen pimakootayk aantravayr lii maansh chi akootayk aandahor lii maansh.

Métis mittens are placed in a mitten box right beside the door. Mittens are given away to travelling friends, relatives, and strangers visiting from afar.

Lii mitenn Michif aashchikataywaa daan enn bwayt di mitenn dret araa la port. Lii mitenn miiyaywuk lii zaamii aan wayaazh ka ayaachik, la paraantii, pi lii zitraanjii ka kiwikaychik wahyow ooshchi.

Christmas is always a treasured time to give someone in your circle a homemade pair of Métis Christmas mittens!

Li zhoor di Nowel tapitow kishchiitayhtaakwun, pi aen boon taan chi miiiyaat awiiyuk daan toon roon enn payr di mitenn Michif di Nowel.

Parts of a Mitten

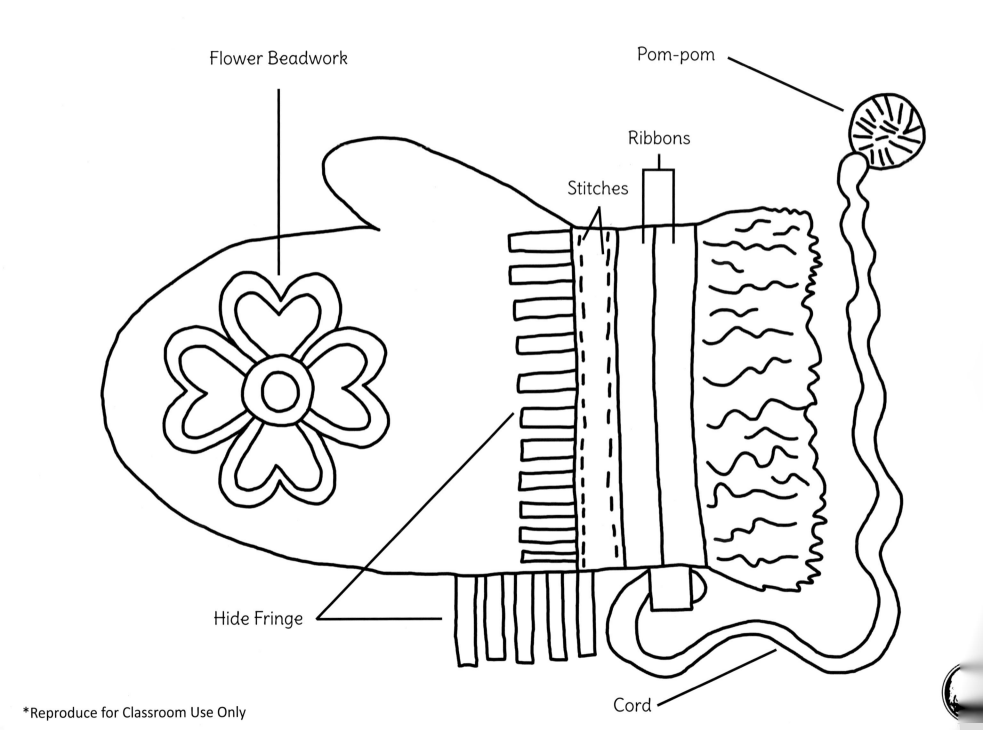

Flower Beadwork

Pom-pom

Ribbons

Stitches

Hide Fringe

Cord

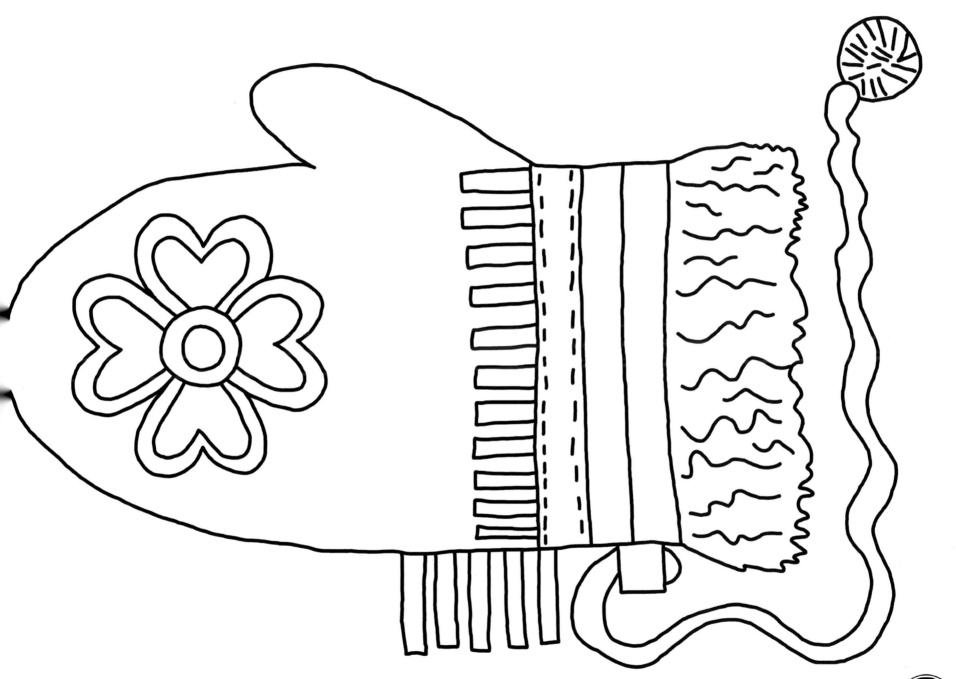

op left: Used with permission from the University of Oregon Museum of Natural and Cultural History
op right and bottom row: Gabriel Dumont Institute Museum Collection

Top left: Beaded mittens by P. Janvier. Photograph by Peter Beszterda. Top right: Mini mittens. Photograph by Peter Beszterda.
Bottom row: Gabriel Dumont Institute Museum Collection

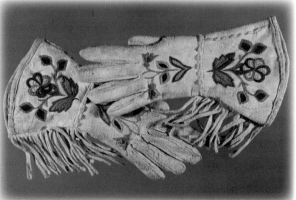

Marii Krismas,

Jwayeu Nowel,

Pi Bonn Aanii

made by Bonnie Hrycuik, Photograph by Peter Beszterda.

Leah Marie Dorion, of Prince Albert, Saskatchewan, is a Métis artist, author, curriculum developer, lecturer, and researcher. For eight years, she was employed in the Gabriel Dumont Institute's Publishing Department as a Curriculum Developer and as Publishing Coordinator. She has written and illustrated several books including *My First Métis Lobstick*, *The Diamond Willow Walking Stick: A Traditional Métis Story About Generosity*, *Relatives With Roots: A Story about Métis Women's Connection to the Land*, and *The Giving Tree: A Retelling of a Traditional Métis Story*. Leah is a visual artist, and an instructor at the Saskatchewan Urban Native Teacher Education Program (SUNTEP) in Prince Albert. For more information about her artistic vision and some of her current creative projects, visit her website at *www.leahdorion.ca*.

Norman Fleury, originally from St. Lazare, Manitoba, is a gifted Michif storyteller and Michif language specialist. He speaks Michif-Cree, Cree, Ojibwa, Dakota, French, and English. Tireless in the promotion and preservation of the Michif-Cree language, he has contributed to dozens of language resources including dictionaries, grammar books, and he has provided innumerable translations for cultural resources. Norman has been employed as a life skills trainer, a university coordinator, a corrections worker, a group home worker, and he served as the executive director of the Brandon Indian and Métis Friendship Centre, and was the Manitoba Métis Federation's Michif Language Program Director. He presently works with the University of Saskatchewan.